HORRID HENRY'S
Car Journey

HORRiD HENRY'S
Car Journey

Francesca Simon
Illustrated by Tony Ross

Orion
Children's Books

Horrid Henry's Car Journey originally appeared in
Horrid Henry and the Bogey Babysitter first published in Great Britain in
2002 by Orion Children's Books
This edition first published in Great Britain in 2011
by Orion Children's Books
a division of the Orion Publishing Group Ltd
Orion House
5 Upper Saint Martin's Lane
London WC2H 9EA
An Hachette UK Company

1 3 5 7 9 10 8 6 4 2

A catalogue record for this book is available from the British Library.

ISBN 978 1 4440 0107 5

Printed by Printer Trento, Italy

www.orionbooks.co.uk
www.horridhenry.co.uk

For Anne, Joel, and Rafael Simon
and all our fights over
who had to sit in the middle

Contents

Chapter 1

"Henry!
We're waiting!"

"Henry! Get down here!"

"Henry! I'm warning you!"

Horrid Henry sat on his bed and
scowled. His mean, horrible parents
could warn him all they liked.
He wasn't moving.

"Henry! We're going to be late,"
yelled Mum.

"Good!" shouted Henry.

"Henry! This is your final warning,"
yelled Dad.

"I don't want to go to Polly's!"
screamed Henry. "I want to go
to Ralph's birthday party."

Mum stomped upstairs.

"Well you can't," said Mum.
"You're coming to the christening,
and that's that."

"NO!" screeched Henry.

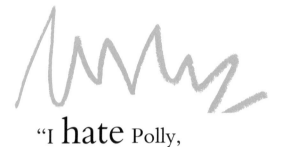

"I hate Polly,

I hate babies,

and I hate you!"

Henry had been a page boy
at the wedding of his cousin,
Prissy Polly, when she'd married
Pimply Paul.

Now they had a prissy,
pimply baby, Vomiting Vera.
Henry had met Vera once before.
She'd thrown up all over him.

Henry had hoped never to see
her again until she was grown up and
behind bars, but no such luck.

He had to go and watch her be dunked in a vat of water, on the same day that Ralph was having a birthday party at Goo-Shooter World.

Chapter 2

Henry had been longing for ages
to go to Goo-Shooter World.
Today was his chance.
His only chance.

But no.
Everything was ruined.

Perfect Peter poked his head
round the door.
"*I'm* all ready, Mum,"
said Perfect Peter.
His shoes were polished,
his teeth were brushed,
and his hair neatly combed.

"I know how annoying it is to be
kept waiting when you're in a rush."

"Thank you, darling Peter,"
said Mum. "At least one of my
children knows how to behave."

Horrid Henry roared and attacked.
He was a swooping vulture digging
his claws into a dead mouse.

"AAAAAAAAEEEEE!"
squealed Peter.

"Stop being horrid, Henry!" said Mum.

"No one told me it was today!"
screeched Henry.

"Yes we did," said Mum.
"But you weren't paying attention."

"As usual," said Dad.

"*I* knew we were going,"
said Peter.

"I DON'T WANT TO GO TO
POLLY'S!" screamed Henry.
"I want to go to Ralph's!"

"Get in the car – NOW!" said Dad.

"Or no TV for a year!" said Mum.

Eeek!

Horrid Henry stopped wailing.
No TV for a year.

Anything was better than that.

Grimly, he stomped down the stairs
and out the front door.
They wanted him in the car.
They'd have him in the car.
"Don't slam the door," said Mum.

SLAM!

Horrid Henry pushed Peter away
from the car door and scrambled for
the right-hand side behind the driver.
Perfect Peter grabbed his legs and
tried to climb over him.
Victory! Henry got there first.

Henry liked sitting on the
right-hand side so he could
watch the speedometer.

Peter liked sitting on the
right-hand side so he could
watch the speedometer.

"Mum," said Peter.
"It's my turn to sit on the right!"

"No it isn't," said Henry.
"It's mine."

"Mine!"

"Mine!"

"We haven't even left and already you're fighting?" said Dad.

"You'll take turns," said Mum. "You can swap after we stop."

Vroom. Vroom.
Dad started the car.
The doors locked.

Chapter 3

Horrid Henry was trapped.
But wait.

Was there a glimmer of hope?
Was there a teeny tiny chance?

What was it Mum always said
when he and Peter were
squabbling in the car?

"If you don't stop fighting
I'm going to turn around
and go home!"

And wasn't home just exactly
where he wanted to be?
All he had to do was to do
what he did best.

"Could I have a story tape, please?"
said Perfect Peter.

"No! I want a music tape,"
said Horrid Henry.

"I want 'Mouse Goes to Town',"
said Peter.

"I want Driller Cannibals'
Greatest Hits," said Henry.

SMACK!
SMACK!
"Waaaaa!"

"Stop it, Henry," said Mum.

"Tell Peter to leave me alone!"
screamed Henry.

"Tell Henry to leave *me* alone!"
screamed Peter.

"Leave each other alone," said Mum.

Horrid Henry glared at
Perfect Peter.

Perfect Peter glared at
Horrid Henry.

Horrid Henry stretched.
Slowly, steadily, centimetre by
centimetre, he spread out into
Peter's area.

"Henry's on my side!"

"No I'm not!"

"Henry, leave Peter alone,"
said Dad. "I mean it."

"I'm not doing anything,"
said Henry. "Are we there yet?"

"No," said Dad.

Thirty seconds passed.

"Are we there yet?"
said Horrid Henry.

"No!" said Mum.

"Are we there yet?"
said Horrid Henry.

"NO!"
screamed Mum and Dad.

"We only left ten minutes ago,"
said Dad.

Ten minutes!

Horrid Henry felt as if they'd
been travelling for hours.

Chapter 4

"Are we a quarter of the way
there yet?"

"NO!"

"Are we halfway there yet?"

"NO!!"

"How much longer until
we're halfway there?"

"Stop it, Henry!" screamed Mum.

"You're driving me crazy!"
screamed Dad.
"Now be quiet and leave us alone."

Henry sighed.
Boy, was this boring. Why didn't
they have a decent car, with built-in
video games, movies, and jacuzzi?

That's just what he'd have,
when he was king.

Softly, he started to hum
under his breath.

"Henry's humming!"

"Stop being horrid, Henry!"

"I'm not doing anything,"
protested Henry.

He lifted his foot.

"MUM!" squealed Peter.
"Henry's kicking me."

"Are you kicking him, Henry?"

"Not yet," muttered Henry.

Then he screamed.

"Mum! Peter's looking out
of my window!"

"Dad! Henry's looking out
of *my* window."

"Peter breathed on me."

"Henry's breathing loud
on purpose."

"Henry's staring at me."

"Peter's on my side!"

"Tell him to stop!"
screamed Henry and Peter.

Mum's face was red.
Dad's face was red.

"That's it!" screamed Dad.

"I can't take this any more!"
screamed Mum.

Yes! thought Henry.
We're going to turn back!

Chapter 5

But instead of turning round,
the car screeched to a halt at
the motorway services.

"We're going to take a break,"
said Mum. She looked exhausted.

"Who needs a wee?" said Dad.
He looked even worse.

"Me," said Peter.

"Henry?"

"No," said Henry.

He wasn't a baby.
He knew when he needed a wee
and he didn't need one now.

"This is our only stop, Henry,"
said Mum. "I think you should go."

"NO!" screamed Henry.
Several people looked up.
"I'll wait in the car."

Mum and Dad were too tired
to argue. They disappeared into
the services with Peter.

Rats.

Despite his best efforts, it looked like Mum and Dad were going to carry on. Well, if he couldn't make them turn back, maybe he could *delay* them? Somehow?

Suddenly Henry had a wonderful, spectacular idea.

It couldn't be easier, and it was guaranteed to work. He'd miss the christening!

Mum, Dad, and Peter got back
in the car. Mum drove off.

"I need a wee," said Henry.

"Not now, Henry."

"I NEED A WEE!"
screamed Henry.
"NOW!"

Mum headed back to the services.
Dad and Henry went to the toilets.

"I'll wait for you outside,"
said Dad.
"Hurry up or we'll be late."

Late!

What a lovely word. Henry went
into the toilet and locked the door.
Then he waited.
And waited. And waited.

Finally, he heard Dad's
grumpy voice.
"Henry? Have you fallen in?"

Henry rattled the door.
"I'm locked in," said Henry.
"The door's stuck. I can't get out."

"Try, Henry," pleaded Dad.

"I have," said Henry.
"I guess they'll have to break
the door down."

That should take a few hours.
He settled himself on the toilet seat
and got out a comic.

"Or you could just crawl
underneath the partition into
the next stall," said Dad.

Aaargghh.

Henry could have burst into tears.
Wasn't it just his rotten luck to try
to get locked in a toilet which had
gaps on the sides?

Henry didn't much fancy wriggling
round on the cold floor.
Sighing, he gave the stall door
a tug and opened it.

Chapter 6

Horrid Henry sat in silence
for the rest of the trip.

He was so depressed he didn't
even protest when Peter
demanded his turn on the right.
Plus, he felt car sick.
Henry rolled down his window.

"Mum!" said Peter. "I'm cold!"

Dad turned the heat on.

"Having the heat on makes me
feel sick," said Henry.

"I'm going
to be sick!"
whimpered
Peter.

"I'm going
to be sick,"
whined Henry.

"But we're almost there,"
screeched Mum.
"Can't you just hold on until . . ."

Bleccchh.

Peter threw up all over Mum.

Blecccchhh.

Henry threw up all over Dad.

The car pulled into the driveway.
Mum and Dad staggered out
of the car to Polly's front door.

"We survived," said Mum, mopping
her dress.

"Thank God that's over,"
said Dad, mopping his shirt.

Horrid Henry scuffed his feet sadly
behind them. Despite all his hard
work, he'd lost the battle.

While Rude Ralph and Dizzy Dave
and Jolly Josh were dashing about
spraying each other with green goo
later this afternoon he'd be stuck
at a boring party with lots of
grown-ups yak yak yaking.

Oh misery!

Ding dong.

The door opened.
It was Prissy Polly. She was in
her bathrobe and slippers.

She carried a stinky, smelly,
wailing baby over her shoulder.

Pimply Paul followed.
He was wearing a filthy T-shirt
with sick down the front.

"Eeeek," squeaked Polly.

Mum tried to look as if she had
not been through hell and barely
lived to tell the tale.

"We're here!" said Mum brightly.
"How's the lovely baby?"

"Too prissy," said Polly.

"Too pimply," said Paul.

Polly and Paul looked at
Mum and Dad.

"What are you doing here?"
said Polly finally.

"We're here for the christening,"
said Mum.

"Vera's christening?" said Polly.

"It's *next* weekend," said Paul.

Mum looked like she wanted
to sag to the floor.

Dad looked like he wanted
to sag beside her.

"We've come on the wrong day?"
whispered Mum.

"You mean, we have to go and
come back?" whispered Dad.

"Yes," said Polly.

"Oh no," said Mum.

"Oh no," said Dad.

"Bleccch," vomited Vera.

"Eeeek!" wailed Polly. "Gotta go."

She slammed the door.

"You mean, we can go home?" said
Henry. "Now?"

"Yes," whispered Mum.

"Whoopee!"

screamed Henry.

"Hang on, Ralph, here I come!"